THE CALL
OF DUTY

The Precinct

The Precinct

Bruce Jones
writer

Tom Mandrake
with David Finch and Art Thibert
artists

Transparency Digital with Avalon Studios
colorists

Randy Gentile with Chris Eliopoulos
letterers

Brian Smith and C. B. Cebulski
associate editors

Ralph Macchio
editor

Joe Quesada
editor in chief

Bill Jemas
president

THE CALL OF DUTY VOL. 2: THE PRECINCT. Contains material originally published in magazine form as THE CALL OF DUTY: THE PRECINCT #1-5. First printing 2003. ISBN# 0-7851-0974-9. Published by MARVEL COMICS, a division of MARVEL ENTERTAINMENT GROUP, INC. OFFICE OF PUBLICATION: 10 East 40th Street, New York, NY 10016. Copyright © 2002 and 2003 Marvel Characters, Inc. All rights reserved. $9.99 per copy in the U.S. and $15.95 in Canada (GST #R127032852); Canadian Agreement #40668537. All characters featured in this issue and the distinctive names and likenesses thereof, and all related indicia are trademarks of Marvel Characters, Inc. No similarity between any of the names, characters, persons, and/or institutions in this magazine with those of any living or dead person or institution is intended, and any such similarity which may exist is purely coincidental. **Printed in Canada.** STAN LEE, Chairman Emeritus. For information regarding advertising in Marvel Comics or on Marvel.com, please contact Russell Brown, Executive Vice President, Consumer Products, Promotions and Media Sales at 212-576-8561 or rbrown@marvel.com

10 9 8 7 6 5 4 3 2 1

Prologue:

"...had a dream..."

"...dreamed I flunked the written..."

...thing is, I was *glad*, Matty.

Happy I flunked. What's that mean-- *Matty*?

I'll start the coffee...

Hey--

Grumpy this morning...

Patient is not grumpy.

You *passed* the test, Gunz, everyone seems to know it but *you*.

So why'd I dream--

Because you're an inward mass of roiling insecurity...despite the outward tough guy facade. Fortunately, you're a great lover.

Eat. You're late.

Not late... just can't argue with my mouth full.

"...roiling"!

Top o' the morning, "Lieutenant" Gunzer!

It's too early, Sammy. In every sense.

They stick me with this Aryan ape, then they promote him.

Uh-oh! *Bigot cop!*

Got a *bigot cop* here, folks!

Freedom of speech, my *kraut* friend! What makes this country great!

And everyone knows you'll get the promotion, so don't start with the modesty crap.

Yeah? Where'd you get the corner on wisdom?

We Jews *are* the corner, where you been?

Oh crap, already! Ain't even had my morning doughnut...

He's got our *daughter!* He's *stone psycho!* Got a *gun!*

Yes, ma'am, take a breath now...

Slowly now... floor and number?

He's gonna shoot Trisha, then *jump!* He's *psycho!*

Wait in the car, please, ma'am.

Two-eleven, two-eleven! Code 3 at Harper and Spring-- apartment 3D, request backup and hostage negotiator!

Hey, we don't *need* that!

I mean it's just *Jimmy Garcia,* right?

Gotta start helpin' with the housework, Jim! Can't have Loretta doin' it all!

Cheatin' tramp! It ain't even my kid!

"House of Usher"! Was that it?

That was *Corman.*

How 'bout we let Trish go, Jim? Then we talk one-on-one! Sound like a plan?

You *hearin'* me, pig? She *ain't* my kid! Look at her! Blonde curls, genius!

Got yer *eyes*, though, Jim! No mistake there! The eyes *don't* lie!

Who's *that?*

Officer *Liebman,* Jim. My *partner.* 'Member?

Blow his Jew head off, man!

Uh-oh! *Bigot!*

Got a bigot psycho here, folks!

Where's the damn negotiator?

Half of Spring is closed. Roadwork. Cover me...

Hey! *I'm* up!

You get promoted today... *I'll* do it.

I *know* him better'n you.

Yeah, I can see yuse is *real close!*

Jimbo! Lookin' good, my man!

Easy, big guy, I ain't packin'...

My daddy is real upset. There's a *war* coming.

Yeah, I know, honey. It's a scary time right now.

Hey?! Where's the little girl you were just with?

We're ready to take the woman driver to--

She was standing *right there!*

She was--?

What little girl?

Little blonde with a flower shirt on! Right there not one second ago!

Little blonde with a flower shirt?

The Precinct

Number 1

Brooklyn...

This is bull, Gunz. How about a taco?

Let's give him a minute, Sammy.

He's had two hours. My hemorrhoids killin' me.

Turn thy other cheek, brother.

Waste a freakin' time.

Hey, I ever tell you that funny story 'bout my first partner?

No, but I gotta strong feelin' yer gonna.

"Young guy. Rookie. Handsome. Shot dead, first day on the force."

"Gee, that is funny."

"So they assign me this new partner. A woman. But I mean a real looker! Casabas out to here!"

"Yeah?"

"I mean, you could not take yer eyes off this broad. Not that she wasn't a good cop 'n all, she was. But it was distractin', ya know?"

"Uh-huh."

So we're driving around, ya know? Doin our job. This was back when a cop occasionally engaged in somethin' besides a drug bust...

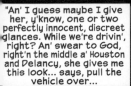

"An' I guess maybe I give her, y'know, one or two perfectly innocent, discreet glances. While we're drivin', right? An' swear to God, right'n the middle a' Houston and Delancy, she gives me this look... says, pull the vehicle over...

"So I'm like-- what gives? An' I pull to the curb and she says, "C'mere, hotshot, an' pulls me into this back alley. An' I'm standin' there, Gunz, in this alley smack in the middle of town, and this broad starts peeling off her blues!"

I'm gawkin' like a freakin idiot, an' this new partner of mine sez: "Take a good look at 'em, Liebman, first and last time! Get yer eyes full. I ain't getting my butt shot off tomorrow on accounta you oglin' these things, unnerstan'?"

Yer kiddin...

Swear to God. Then she--

Chill, Sammy. We got movement...

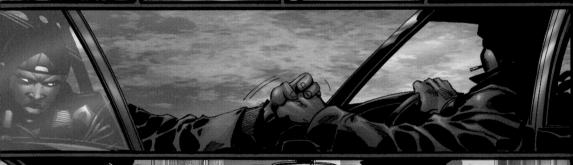

That's a hand-off, let's do it!

Two-eleven, two-eleven! We have touch-down!

SHREEEEEEEEEEEEEE!

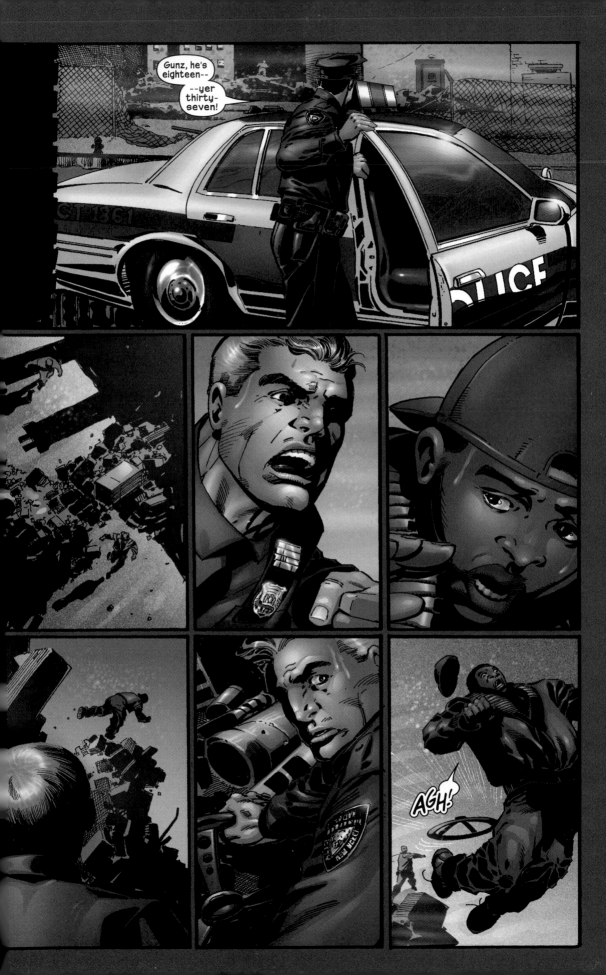

WHUMP!

:pant pant:
What's a hurry, Tito?

Got a mid-term final or something?

Ain't done nothin', mutha! Got nothin' on me!

Nothin', huh?

What's this in yer fist, Tito? Snickers bar?!

Yo-- want my attorney present! You hear me?

Drop it, you little punk, before I forget my good manners!

Police harassment! Yo, officer molestin' a minor here!

Moments later, back at the car...

We got set up, Sammy. Slickern' owl snot.

What the hell's this--?

A diversion? I shoulda seen it. Too easy. Damn.

We get decoyed away from the real transaction, and Tito is back on the street in twelve hours... juvies always are. We were suckered, Sammy boy.

Just another day in paradise. So what now? Taco Bell?

SKREEE

I wanna price some antiques first...

CRASSHHH!

...oh, man! Don't do that!

ANTIQUES

Did I do that? Geez, I am so clumsy!

Bull in a china shop, my wife says!

Man, I gots to pay for that!

Ornel, check it out. Am I getting fat you think--?

Hey, man, watch it!

C'mon, guys, you gonna get my butt fired!

Reason I ask is, I been eatin' a lot a Snickers lately, know what I mean, Ornel? Friend of yers named Tito been givin' em to me. What's that about you think?

Look man, I tole you everything I know! I ain't messin' wit'cha this time!

This time, huh...?

Hey, Sam--

--this clock look on time to you?

No, man, don't do that!

You say something, Gunz?

Damn, bitch!

CRASH!

Uh-oh! The B word!

Excuse me--?

N-Nothin', man! I-I didn' mean it!

Ever see a crack baby, Ornel? Screamin' and cryin' snot all day from the habit he's born with?

And that's the lucky ones. Some don't make a sound at all. Twelve years later they ain't made a sound yet... somebody's feeding 'em with a spoon and still cleanin' their diapers.

A name, Ornel. A real name, this time--

--or the next thing that breaks won't glue back!

Cleon Lincoln! Got braided hair, no front teeth! Only you didn't get it from me! He'll kill me, man! Sucka's crazy!

We'll be discreet. Just tell me where he hangs.

You ain't gonna believe me! Cleon, he done got religio

Church of the Holy Spirit...

Forgive me, Father, for I have sinned...

What do you want, Frank?

Givin' yer blessing to bangers now, Joey?

All are welcome in the Lord's house, Frankie.

Yeah? Whad he confess to, stealin' a candy bar?

So?

The same.

Well, I gotta go chase bad guys...

Would it kill you to light a candle for someone? Donate a buck?

I gave at the office.

Hey! You should go see Pop. It's been months.

Aww, Joey... he don't even know me, for chrissake.

You damned hypocrite! Why don't you just admit it makes you uncomfortable?

Hypocrite?

Me, Joey? Me?

Whatever...

Long Island, the Sunnyside Nursing Home...

--an' Sammy's just standing there in the alley gawkin', and this new partner of his starts peelin' outta her blues...

"Take a good look!", she says, "First time and last! I ain't getting shot on the job on account of youse gawkin' at my hooters!"

How about that, Pop? Can you beat that?

That Sammy, huh?

...yeah, that Sammy... ol' Sammy...

Mr. Gunzer?

Time for our meds!

Okay, Pop. You hang in there, huh? No pinchin' the nurses.

We get along just fine! He's my little tiger!

Yeah, lady? Shoulda seen him when he was a cop.

Brooklyn...

T-Trisha...?

I... I'm scared... for my daddy...

RRRRRIIIIII

IINNNGGG!

Agh!

...yeah.

Where? Yeah, yeah-- give me five.

I don't understand, isn't this a job for the narcs? You're not even officially a detective until next week.

It's a kid, Matty. A DOA. They think he may be one of my contacts.

KNOX BUILDING,
UNDERGROUND PARKING

Gunz! Peace officer's work is never done, huh?

Hey, man, I already ID'd him. It's Ornel...

You don't have to look at that mess...

Come on, man... I'll buy you a drink...

It wasn't our fault, Gunz! The little punk was in way over his head!

He came running out of the garage you say?

Yessir, running and screaming! Second later, another kid charges out, runs the other way... only he wasn't on fire!

Doesn't add up, Sam...

What doesn't? It's a gang hit, pure and simple.

When was the last time you saw a gang retaliation involving fire?

I'm telling ya, Sammy... there's a screw loose here somewhere...

Brooklyn, The Coney Island Amusement Park...

You jealous?

Of the blonde? Nah, he's just being big brother like he does with you.

His job... now *that* I get jealous of.

He called me a hypocrite, did you know?

Gunz? Joey, no!

Actually I called him one first, but that's not the point.

Ever wonder why I quit the force, Matty? Three generations of Gunzer cops, and I'm the first to quit. Ever wonder about that?

I really never considered it my bus--

Because I was scared.

That's it. That's the whole of it. I was plain scared.

I told him, Matty. Not long after I quit. I told Gunz it was because I was scared.

What... did he say?

He said: "Only stupid cops aren't scared. That ain't a reason."

And he's right. You're suppose to work behind church doors, Matty, not hide behind them.

Funny, huh?

I expected him to call me coward. I'd have accepted that.

"Hypocrite" though... That's a heavy cross to bear...

Church of the Holy Spirit...

...I've lost my faith, Father...

...and the terror of it is, I don't know if I ever had it!

Help me, Lord... tell me what I must do... give me a sign...

...any sign!

...help me, Father...

...people will die... like at the Knox building...

Father--?

D-Did... did you see her?

See who, Father? We just come to do a little soul searchin'!

You been practicin'.

Vic Tanny's gym, every Thursday night for six years.

What brought you around?

Well, the sudden influx of converted gangbangers as a start...

...still, it took me a while to catch on to it.

You have to look close...

...third row from the top, what do you see?

Candles.

And they're making you a detective?

Second from the left. Not quite the shade of red as the others. More a dark orange, see it?

Think of the table as a grid... a city map.

Houston Street there... Bales Avenue there... Cole Street over there...

The dealer moves around the candle to mark the next drop site... the runner reads the site at his next "confession."

Dealer never meets runner. Cops never catch either.

Smart.

The Precinct

Number 2

AGHHHH!

Gunz! Honey!

Sorry... nightmare...

My God, sweetheart, you're soaked!

Honey? Where are you going?

Need some air... gonna take a little drive...

At three in the morning!

Go back to sleep, honey. I'll be right back.

UNDERGROUND PARKING

Yo, Checkers. Slits here. Target just passed.

But we got a problem.

There's another guy drivin'. Looks like a priest. You said there'd be only the cop and the woman.

So what's yo problem, dawg? Adjust accordingly.

No disrespect, but you sure you're down wif this hit, man? I mean, this cop Gunzer's gotta local hero thing goin', you dig? Up for all kina promotions and stuff...

He keeps sniffin' round that Knox Building in Manhattan where Ornel was capped!

Thought you said nobody on the circuit knows who did Ornel?! So what's this cop gonna find to hurt you?

He's messin wif my turf, fool! Now you gonna off Deputy Dawg there, or I gotta call in a real pro?

It's cool, baby, it's cool! He's history! On my way!

VA-ROOoOMMM!

Love your brother's car, but I go nowhere until I've had a hot bath and scoured off the road dust!

Nice cabins!

C'mon, little brother, let's take a walk...

Relax, we're not going to the damn carnival...

...yet.

I'm a little tired, Frankie. You walk. I'll hang around and watch Matty take a bath.

Listen, Joey, about the little angel girl, Matty do--

Glad you brought that up. I've got a theory about our mysterious little girl...

I think she knows us.

How can that be, if we don't know her?

It ain't me I'm scared for.

I been havin' crazy dreams, Joey... all kinda death symbology...

I think maybe somethin's gonna happen to me... who's gonna take care of Matty if I take it in the shorts?

Frankie, death images don't necessarily mean dying... sometimes it can be a metaphor for change.

Somethin's comin', Joey... somethin' big...

...I'm gonna lose Matty... I can feel it inside...

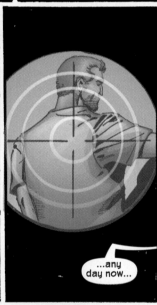

...any day now...

Sorry, sir, going to have to ask you to stay on the trail...

...trying to keep the area as pristine as possible!

Thanks, officer, won't happen again.

Enjoy your stay!

See if Matty's ready, huh?

I'll get tickets for the carnival!

--oh!

Matty... Sorry! Damn.

C'mon, Joey, I've got a swimsuit smaller than this.

Besides, we're practically brother and sister!

Not to me, Matty...

Joey...?

Joey! Why didn't you... ever...

Frankie saw you first. And by high school I'd made up my mind about the faith, so...

Aw who am I kidding? I was terrified of women. Scared of failure. Just like I was scared of failing at being a cop.

Since PS fifty-one, kiddo. Right through the heart.

I'm quitting the priesthood, did Frankie tell you?

No! Joey!

Don't talk a whole lot for a married couple, do you?

I suppose not.

Sweetie! Is there anything I can do?

I guess what's done is done.

Right?

A carnival in the woods! I guess the scenery and wildlife aren't entertaining enough, right?

Let's ride the coaster first!

I *hate* roller coasters!

He's afraid of heights.

How about the Merry-Go-Round?!

Afraid of circles, too?

uhh!

Gunz!

Oh, God! He's having a heart attack!

He's been shot!

...black kid... Slits Johnson... leather jacket... eagle...

Resort desk? We have a man shot... I need a Medvac team immediately! At the southeast carnival entrance! Yes!

...go get him, Joey... don't let me die like... this...

Joey!

NO!

STOP THAT MAN!

Damnit! Where'd you go?!

...c'mon... c'mon...

...show yourself...

Hey! We were here first!

Shut up, fool!

All hands inside the cars, please!

Hey, man! Are you nuts?!

He's got a gun!

Drop it, Slits!

BLAM!

Hang on, honey... the medics are on their way!

Hey... ya wanna get offa me, please. Can't breathe.

Gunz?

S'all the fuss about?

Little nick in the lumbar... needed to lose some weight there anyway...

Wanna give me a hand here, honey...

Across your smart-ass face!

"Nick"?!

Your brother's risking his life with your gun and you're only *nicked*?!

Get off your phony butt right now and go help him!

I am helping him, Matty...

...I am helping him.

Sure! Take five seconds, padre... ...best make it a good prayer!

EEEEEEEEEEEEEEEEEEEEEEEEEEEE

KER-UNCH

It was.

Hey, bro! You gonna hang around here all day?

Joey!

Honey, are you all right?

...G--Gunz is fine... t-turns out it was only a scratch...

Yeah? Only a scratch, huh?

CRACK!

So. How did it feel?

Clipping you? Great!

Catching the bad guy, I mean.

Oh, that... ...yeah... that wasn't bad either!

Brooklyn...

NO!

Wha? ...uh?

Knox Building... don't make... sense... zzzzz

Gunz? Honey, wake up! Gunz!

Wha? Somethin' wrong, Matty?

Gunz, I need to talk! I had a dream!

Dream?

Brooklyn...

Okay, it's almost five... let's do it.

I still got two minutes to talk you *out* of this, Frankie...

Sam, the guy nearly got my brother *killed* comin' after me!

How long 'til he goes after *Matty?!*

No way, pal. This punk Checkers Freeman is goin' *down!*

I'm not sayin' don't go *after* the slime... just do it by the *book!*

Thanks, I *read* that book.

You got a major promotion comin' next week, Frankie...

You gonna risk all that over one lousy scumbag?

Hurry! Guy's *bustin'* up the joint!

A scumbag we already *know* uses the Knox Building as a drop-off? Yeah... for *that* and for my *family.*

Why this obsession with the Knox Building? What're you--

Frankie?

S'matta?

Nuthin'...

Yer up, slugger.

Don't go nowhere, Frankie-- I ain't through wit chew!

Excuse me, sir... going to have to ask you to--

KE-RAISHHHH!

Sir, striking an officer of the law is a felony...

...also there's the pain...

Matty? It's Gunz. Listen, do me a *favor*, huh?

Drop by the church this evening and see my brother, could you?

Joey--? W-Why? What's wrong, Gunz?

Probably nothing. I'm just a little worried about him... you know... him threatening to quit the priesthood an' all.

Church Of The Holy Spirit, Brooklyn...

Matty Gunzer, Father... Joey Gunzer's sister-in-law?

Is the reverend around today?

You didn't know...?

Father Joey retired from the church yesterday.

It was such a blow to all of us. He offered no explanation, but...

...as I'm sure you *know*, a robust, *virile* young man like Father Gunzer, well...

...good looks can be a *mixed* blessing in the priesthood...

I don't suppose it blasphemous to admit that more than a few of our young female parishioners attended service solely on the strength of his... *charisma.*

Do you have his *home* address on Spring?

He...

...*what?!*

Spring Street, Brooklyn...

Joey--?

It's me, Matty!

Door's open-- are you in the shower--?

Damn!

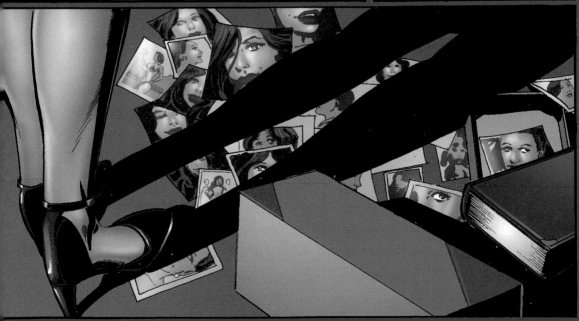

"...once inside you come down this foyer to the sunken living room. Checkers likes girls, so you'll see a lot of 'em but remember why you came. Goon number two will be waiting there, seated on this white divan...

"...white guy named Cletes... likes Brooks Brothers jackets and Czech Army 7.62's-- s'pposed to be a good shot but twitchy...

I'm Sizemore... here to see Checkers Freeman.

Stand there.

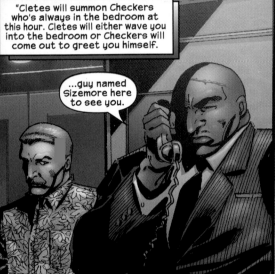

"Cletes will summon Checkers who's always in the bedroom at this hour. Cletes will either wave you into the bedroom or Checkers will come out to greet you himself.

...guy named Sizemore here to see you.

"If you get into the bedroom all you got to worry about is Checkers' chrome-plated Smith & Wesson 624 strapped to his ankle... get past that, out the bedroom window and yer home free.

"If Checkers comes out to see you... well, there's a Spectre 9mm submachine hidden behind the bar over here... but I don't know how the hell you're going to get to it..."

Sizemore to see Mr. Freeman...

Grab the lintel.

--I-I wasn't prying, Joey...I knocked it over by accident...

Don't apologize, Matty. I'm the weirdo with the Matty Gunzer photo gallery here.

One more black spot for the church, eh? Just what it needs these days...

Joey... I... don't know what to say... I'm flattered, but...

You know exactly what to say... you're just too sweet to say it...one of the many reasons I've been in love with you all these years.

Joey, I-

Don't worry. I've decided to return to police work, Matty. Effective immediately. I'm looking at some offers in L.A...

L.A.? But that's so...

Far away? From you? Exactly.

Gunz needs you now, Matty, more than ever. Despite the movies and TV shows, detective work is mostly long hours of paperwork and warming your butt in front of a computer screen.

Gunz needs to be out in the traffic, every day. He doesn't want this new job. Those kinds of responsibilities.

Only he's afraid to admit it ...to you, and to himself.

--oughta keep that bedroom *window* locked, Checkers!

Now hear this...

...you ever *send* one of your goons *near* my partner or his family again, I take you off at the *neck*-- got that, chubby?

Thanks for not getting "*involved*."

Can we go home now?

Hate these snobby Manhattan apartments...

Later...

Hey, man... you're bleeding...

Never mind. Turn left here...

What're you doin'? Hospital's that way!

May as well check on the Knox Building 'long as we're in the neighborhood...

The Precinct

Number 4

Mostly you just try to get through the day... and come out a live Brooklyn cop.

Some days you win. Some you lose.

In the end, it's family that really counts.

That's most days. Occasionally it gets weird. Occasionally nothing makes sense...

When you're sharing road with the best en and EMS workers York has to offer.

Sometimes all the training, all the experience, all the days and nights of risking your butt, just don't count for squat.

Father Joey Gunzer's apartment, Brooklyn.

Mmm...

Wow. I've waited weeks for that.

I've waited years.

Matty...

No... Don't, Joey...

One more word will talk me out of it...

Hey!

They're out!

THEY'RE OUT!

I don't suppose... I mean... Sam--

I'm sorry, Officer... Frank.

Frankie!

Frankie, are you all right?

Yeah... hot there for a while though.

For you guys too, huh?

The Precinct

Ever since I can remember, I wanted to be a Brooklyn cop... me and my little brother Joey.

As a kid, for the *action*, I guess. As an adult... well... for the *pride*.

When we weren't playing cops, we were watching movies. The Rialto on Brooklyn Ave... Saturday matinees... and *always* science fiction.

I finally got to be the cop I always *dreamed* about. Even got some of the science fiction as a bonus...

Also got the wife I always *dreamed* about in Matty. And Joey... well, he quit the force to become a priest. Didn't see that one coming.

Sometimes you miss what's *right* in front of you.

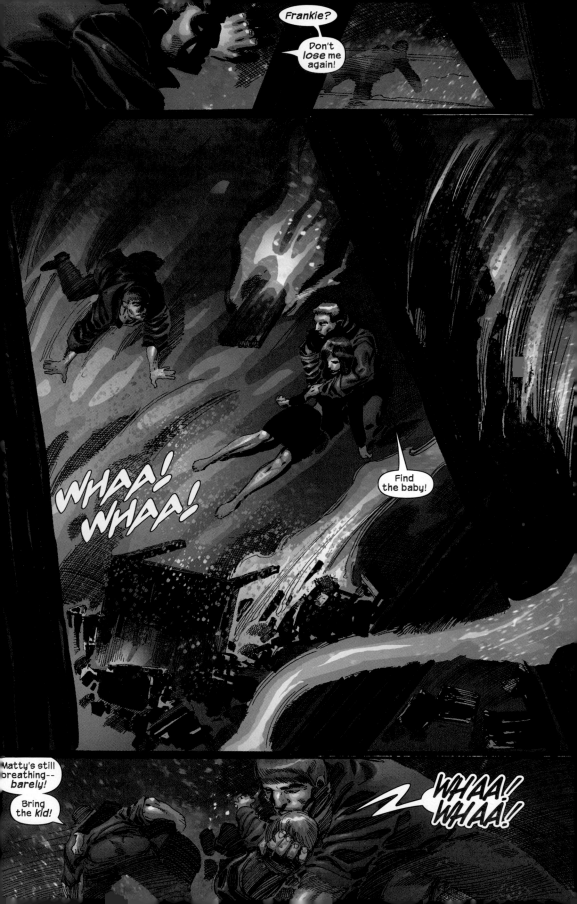

WHUMPP!

Good vitals for *both* of them, Sergeant!

They'll be *fine* once their lungs clear!

You comin'?

No...

You can take care of her from here.

WWEEEEEEE... WHUP! WHUP! WHUP!

EMERGENCY SERVICES

Next:
The Call